How Many Times?

Experimental Fictions

Rhys Hughes

How Many Times?
by Rhys Hughes
ISBN: 978-1-908125-60-6

Publication Date: March 2018

www.eibonvalepress.co.uk

Acknowledgements

Many thanks to Kevin Bufton who first suggested that I write a piece consisting of six paragraphs, each paragraph consisting of six sentences, each sentence consisting of six words. I wrote that short piece (the one that begins 'Six diced carrots in the pot.') but I also wrote five others to make six in total and linked them together to form one story. That's how 'Half a Dozen of the Other' was generated, and this story led to 'The Five Pillars of Flimflam' and then 'Seven Sulky Sides for Seven Bulky Brooders'.

Regards to Mihalis Moulakis who translated my first grid story 'I Entered the Forest at Midnight' into Greek for publication in Παίζουμε λογοτεχνία; (which means "Shall we Play Literature?"), an anthology of OuLiPo texts that appeared in Athens in early 2016. Translating OuLiPo texts is extremely difficult and a prospect that makes most translators blanch. Mihalis handled the difficulties with the panache and skill of Odysseus sailing between the clashing Cyanean Rocks, the rocks in this case being words and meanings. Huge thanks also to Achilleas Kyriakidis, the editor of the anthology, who invited me to contribute.

'Boolean Amours' appeared in the Salò Press anthology *Milk* published in 2017 edited by Sophie Essex and once again I wish to express my gratitude.

Contents

$$(1^4 + 2^4 + 3^4 + 4^4 + 5^4) + 6^4 + 7^4$$

Foreword

I am an enthusiast for experimental fiction, a type of literature that has generally fallen out of favour in recent years. In fact I regard the mid 1970s as the period when it first began its long decline. Suddenly people became impatient with odd typographical layouts, unusual structuring, narrative tricks. Samuel Delany was warned by his publisher not to produce another novel like *Dhalgren*, despite the fact it had sold a million copies, because the public had lost its taste for difficult books. Readers no longer wanted to labour at deciphering a text. Immersion was more important to them now, the main aim of fiction became entertainment and unconventional form was seen as an impediment to a story and its flow, and not an enhancer of the overall literary experience.

Not that experimental fiction vanished completely; it merely became a niche concern, and the idea that a mainstream novel might have holes cut in its pages, so that a reader can glimpse future events (such as the death of a character) and be psychologically prepared for them when they properly arrive, would come to appear ludicrous and perverse. And yet B.S. Johnson's *Albert Angelo*, won fame for just such an innovative technique, and motivated other authors to expand the boundaries of form. But progressive form revealed itself to be a passing fashion rather than a sustainable process in the minds of the publishing industry. Subject matter took precedence over everything. The wildest stories could be told in the most conventional prose and that was enough.

Certain groupings of authors and readers remained eager to experiment, for instance the OuLiPo devotees mainly based in France, but experimental fiction as a commercial concern was dead. In the 1960s, Richard Brautigan's eccentric metafictional masterpiece *Trout Fishing in America* sold two million copies, but it is unlikely that such a book would sell more than a few hundred in the market of today. Those who still persist with experimental fiction tend to regard it as an unprofitable hobby rather than a means of earning royalties. Occasionally books powered by unorthodox form will attain transient success as novelty items, but the label 'experimental fiction' is now synonymous with lack of coherence. This is a shame and narrows the scope of creativity.

The following experimental text originated with the casual suggestion by a reader interested in unusual fiction that I try to compose a tale made up of six paragraphs, each paragraph consisting of six sentences, each sentence formed from six words. I accepted the challenge but composed six tales instead of just one, linked them all together and gave them a six-word title that alluded to the number six. It remains my most sixual story.

The outcome was that a new project was conceived in which my 6x6x6x6 tale would be only one part. I would write more material and link everything together to develop a numerically incremental narrative. I would begin with a 1x1x1x1 piece and gradually progress to a 7x7x7x7 work. The latter, despite the hellishness of its creation, remains my most sevenly story. The individual titles contain as many words as the integers that structure the tales they represent. The point of experimental fiction is that one must never cheat with the rules and the rules are there to make the author's life difficult.

The text I call '$(1^4+2^4+3^4+4^4+5^4) + 6^4 + 7^4$' can therefore be read as a single story or as three linked tales or as a loose series of self-contained fragments. As is always the case with the imposition of an arbitrary but rigorous mathematical structure on a work of fiction, the rhythm of the prose is not that of the writer's natural voice. There are both hazards and boons to this method. The flow might be hampered, the progression seem stilted. On the other hand, the discipline can force a writer to break out of patterns that have become overfamiliar, bland and too comfortable, and to generate prose that features original imagery and unique notions that might never have appeared without the creative constraints imposed on the mind by the work's precise requirements.

The Five Pillars of Flimflam

Good (1x1x1x1)

Morning.

Breakfast Time (2x2x2x2)

Burnt toast. Apricot jam.
    Grapefruit juice. Weak tea.

Boiled noses. Spider legs.
    Grilled elbows. Robot nuts.

Off to Work (3x3x3x3)

In the car. Down the road. Through the tunnel.
    River flows above. Bright light ahead. The other side.
    Find parking space. Enter the building. Up the stairs.

Early start today. Boss is angry. Bad office atmosphere.
    I know why. Economy in trouble. Possible job losses.
    Must try harder. Keep head down. Escape the axe.

He comes in. Face very sour. Lower lip trembling.
    Blood will flow. Elevates his hand. Points a finger.
    Picks a victim. "To the guillotine!" Nasty paper cut.

One of These Days (4x4x4x4)

Killing employees is new. Never been done before. But times are changing. Work is getting harder.

The boss is unrepentant. I don't blame him. He is under pressure. From his own boss.

Smith was very unlucky. He was chosen randomly. His head comes back. Planted on his desk.

It won't grow there. Will just slowly decay. Features eventually drop off. A warning to us.

I need to escape. Find a better life. One of these days. Or else go mad.

Not an easy task. Most dreams are futile. But I am determined. I will succeed eventually.

Deception is the answer. Fake my own death. Find a new identity. Abandon all my responsibilities.

Must forget my wife. Toughen my aching heart. Fossilize the damn organ. That's the only option.

Where shall I go? I consult an atlas. Somewhere quiet and remote. An obscure tropical island.

Not easy getting there. I need a boat. Can dead eyes mock? Smith's gaze is penetrating.

Take me with you. His features demand it. Or I will tell. Blackmailed by a head!

I nod my assent. The dead eyes close. I study the furniture. A large filing cabinet.

A pair of scissors. I stand and run. Stab the water cooler. The full tank ruptures.

Drinking water gushes out. Office is quickly flooded. Doors burst wide open. Waterfall down the stairs.

Filing cabinet is empty. I push it over. Floats like a cork. I jump onto it.

Caught by the current. Holding Smith's head tightly. We shoot the rapids. Out onto the street.

Two Heads Better than One (5x5x5x5)

At last we spy land. Or at least I do. Smith's eyes have gone off. Went off without telling me. Shrivelled in the hot sun.

Lost at sea for months. My country left far behind. A society changing too rapidly. Robots will soon take over. It was time to leave.

But not easy being adrift. The filing cabinet is leaking. I am bailing it out. My wallet is nearly empty. Soon be swamped and sink.

The lonely island looms ahead. Waves pound a sloping beach. I resign myself to destiny. Washed up by the surf. I am now a castaway.

Drag myself over the sand. Smith's head rolls back down. Let it fend for itself. Let it make new friends. With sharks in the deep.

Life must always go on. I construct a simple shelter. I dwell in the jungle. I pluck the freshest fruits. Drink the purest spring water.

Aeroplanes cross the azure dome. High above my marooned head. Full of workers on vacation. My holiday will be endless. I have resigned from worry.

But worry hasn't forgotten me. Something falls from the sky. A bottle containing a message. An aeroplane has dropped it. I carefully extract the paper.

I recognise the hurried scrawl. "I have been watching you." The words of my boss. It is clearly a threat. He wants me to return.

I refuse to go back. Robot nuts for breakfast again? I would rather drown myself. I will resist with passion. I slowly eat the note.

My island should be fortified. An attack can be expected. My past is my adversary. It is coming for me. But I will be prepared.

I sharpen branches into stakes. Plant them firmly in sand. Construct a number of traps. I fashion sharp stone axes. They are not very fashionable.

I practice at throwing spears. Make a bow and arrows. I become a deadly shot. Fruit on trees are targets. Juice splatters like enemy gore.

My muscles expand every day. A reborn child of nature. I am fast and tough. All five senses more acute. I have abandoned civilised sloth.

When will the invasion come? I scan the horizon carefully. Waiting for the landing craft. Gaze at the immense sky. Watching for the parachute troops.

But my boss is sneaky. He is also supremely nasty. He won't delegate this task. It is a personal mission. He will kill me himself.

And there is no warning. He erupts from the ground. He is piloting a mole. A mechanical digger of steel. The spiral drill whirls menacingly.

He leaps from the cockpit. His face purple with rage. A three piece bulletproof suit. My spear bounces harmlessly off. "To the guillotine with you!"

He wields an unusual weapon. Oblique blade on a chain. Lop heads at a distance. I duck just in time. The force fells a tree.

I retreat out of range. But he keeps pursuing me. I represent everything he despises. I have escaped from prison. The dungeon of modern existence.

To teach me a lesson. That is his urgent desire. And to set an example. To discourage others from fleeing. He will show no mercy.

I stumble along the beach. The blade revolves even faster. Now he can scent victory. What does victory smell like? Not at all like napalm.

Burnt toast and apricot jam. Boiled noses and spider legs. In other words like breakfast! The surf drums the sand. I fall to the ground.

Have tripped over a pebble. My boss utters a laugh. Something round is washed ashore. It rolls up the beach. Carried by momentum and willpower.

The malformed head of Smith! It bites his evil ankles. Gnaws his feet clean off. My boss screams in agony. And slowly he is devoured.

Half a Dozen of the Other
(6x6x6x6)

Six diced carrots in the pot. Four sliced potatoes and two missionaries. Spices and herbs in small amounts. That is the simple traditional recipe. I don't want to alter it. I am a conservative tribal chieftain.

The dicing of vegetables is risky. An activity I try to avoid. But someone needs to do it. We still use a stone axe. A clumsy tool for the kitchen. But custom shouldn't be argued with.

Occasionally there is a bad accident. The stone axe misses its target. Instead of carrots, legs are chopped. Into the pot with the limbs! Waste not, want not, they say. The oldest sayings are the wisest.

I have been lucky so far. I have lost no body parts. I am skilled with an axe. Because I used to play guitar. At least that's what I believe. Heavy music on a stone guitar.

Chopped legs and guitars are tasty. But missionaries are much more nourishing. They come here year after year. They clearly don't mind being eaten. They are very good-natured people. They stand in the pot smiling.

True, those smiles are rather forced. At least they make an effort. They gamble with the diced carrots. They throw them like real dice. To pass the time while boiling. But nobody ever wins any bets.

I was born in the 1960s. Near the end of that decade. Almost everyone spoke in hippy slang. But I was very literal minded. Because I was still a baby. I didn't understand figures of speech.

My father was a neglectful man. He never looked after his children. We had to fend for ourselves. I found a physical labouring job. I had to earn my keep. I was only eighteen months old.

I excavated three large shipping canals. I couldn't even talk properly yet. I dug one hundred irrigation channels. I still cried for my mama. I sunk a dozen mine shafts. I sucked my thumb between jobs.

My work colleagues usually avoided me. They didn't like working with babies. It reflected badly on their reputations. Even the foreman left me alone. I burrowed a vast underground bunker. I was paid in bottled milk.

Finally I tunnelled under the river. I did this for the traffic. It saved commuters many frustrating hours. I should have been a hero. I should have received a bonus. Been interviewed on radio and television.

But I was given the sack. There had been a big misunderstanding. "You dig, baby," wasn't an instruction. It was just more hippy slang. How was I expected to know? My efforts had been in vain.

My friend was leaving the country. He was always my best friend. I didn't want him to go. But he had a job offer. I couldn't try to stop him. I felt a sadness at parting.

"Keep me posted," I told him. "Are you sure?" he asked me. "Nothing I'd like better," I said. My friend always kept his word. Certainly he would keep me posted. I waved goodbye on the platform.

His train soon left the station. So I decided to go home. It was late, I was tired. I went to bed to sleep. I woke late the next morning. Someone was knocking on the door.

I got up and answered it. Burly men stood there before me. They grabbed hold of me roughly. They bundled me into an envelope. A very large padded manila envelope. I struggled but to no avail.

The envelope was a strong one. I couldn't manage to burst it. My assailants had sealed it tight. I felt myself being carried outside. Where might they be taking me? To the Post Office in fact.

I was weighed and paid for. A great many stamps were required. To what address was I mailed? The Setting Sun, is the answer. They mailed me to the sunset. I would circle the world forever.

I was captain of a ship. We sailed north, south, east, west. On six of the seven seas. I didn't like the seventh sea. That was one sea too many. I was an old grizzled sailor.

I had witnessed many strange things. One evening I heard a shout. "Iceberg ahead!" came the anxious cry. A lookout had seen the danger. A huge floating mountain of ice. It was a very foggy night.

I ordered the engines to stop. But it was already too late. Our momentum kept us going forward. We were on a collision course. Then I saw the dreaded iceberg. There was something odd about it.

Another ship was trapped inside it. Encased in the hard glittering ice! It was a ship like mine. Identical in even the smallest detail. Perfectly preserved in its icy tomb. The sight was an astonishing one.

My own ship struck the iceberg. But then the iceberg suddenly shattered. It broke into a million pieces. How was such a thing possible? Jagged shards landed on my deck. I went to pick one up.

It was not ice but glass. The iceberg was a giant bottle. The other ship was now free. As we sank, it sailed off. A man waved from its deck. He was me, writing this now.

I stopped moving at long last. I still couldn't see a thing. I was very hungry and thirsty. I hadn't eaten for many weeks. My bones and joints were stiff. It had been a tough journey.

I wondered where I might be. Then the envelope was ripped open. Had I reached the Setting Sun? This seemed to be extremely unlikely. I blinked in the bright light. My eyes were now very sensitive.

A man was looking at me. He was strong, tall and imposing. He was dressed in feathered robes. Was he a chieftain, I wondered? I was on a tropical island. I'd been lost in the mail.

Such an occurrence is not unusual. Many parcels go missing in transit. I was clearly one such example. I crawled out of the envelope. My muscles were feeble and wasted. Rather unsteadily, I managed to stand.

17

"Are you a missionary?" he asked. I told him that I wasn't. He seemed rather disappointed by this. "Can you dice carrots?" he persisted. I replied that yes, I could. "With a stone axe?" he added.

I was willing to try anything. I was happy to be free. I diced six carrots very clumsily. The axe was hard to use. I accidentally chopped off my leg. The chieftain congratulated me for this.

I am tired of the ocean. I want to explore a river. The change will do me good. I hated being inside that bottle. The ocean is a dangerous place. Rivers are surely a lot safer.

Here is the mouth of one. I like the look of it. I give the order to turn. We are sailing up the river. How far will it take us? It will be a nice surprise.

That lucky collision rescued my ship. The other captain has probably drowned. I feel quite bad about that. But it is not my fault. It was a very foggy night. Accidents happen, that's the simple truth.

My crew like to play games. They prefer to gamble with dice. They carve dice from root vegetables. The river mouth licks its lips. That is a metaphor, of course. The vegetables are not that tasty.

This river has a strange appearance. I don't believe it is natural. I now think it is artificial. But who could have dug it? A figure sits on the bank. It clutches a spade very tightly.

It is just a little baby. It is surrounded by burly workmen. Each one holds a padded envelope. They wear expressions of dark menace. Quick, where is the remote control? I really need to change canals.

Seven Sulky Sides for Seven Bulky Brooders
(7x7x7x7)

The first brooder is known as Mun. He sits on a little brown stool. His chin rests in his clenched fist. He knows this is a classic pose. And there are other classical things nearby. Doric columns hold up the heavy roof. Mun is a pillar of the community.

A long time ago he was bald. Then hair began growing on his head. Also on the entirety of his body. Maybe he was bitten by a werewolf. He won't be drawn on the matter. He will only be sketched with crayons. Nobody can explain why this should be.

He plays chess with some noble qualities. Grace, for example, and an unexpected fluidity. But Grace prefers backgammon in the evenings. She isn't here tonight at the tournament. Mun must face his opponents by himself. He is certainly up to the task. He has all the fluidity he needs.

The finest players of backgammon are owls. That myth has still never been disproved. Mun believes it because it amuses him. But chess is his bread and butter. Not that he cares much for sandwiches. He prefers the company of coral warlocks. They cast spells to help him win.

The key to every warlock is bent. That's why it's tricky to open them. Inside, they have skeletons of black glass. Coral warlocks tie themselves in reef knots. Sandwiches just drift in the offshore wind. That is the main difference between them. Grace is not any kind of witch.

She's a mayor in her spare time. She rules a village of sad people. They always grumble about the bad weather. Buck up your ideas, she tells them! They prance like donkeys and kick hard. Mun has no interest in such activities. Chess for him is the purest politics.

He is brooding on his next move. The little brown stool creaks under him. Finally he makes a rather bold decision. He slides the bishop across the board. It is now deep in enemy territory. It's going to be a long night. Only one move per day is permitted.

The second brooder is known as Tue. His mouth is always munching on something. If not food, then his own tongue. He doesn't ever swallow what he chews. It's just a nervous habit for him. Mastication is his way of expressing cogitation. He sometimes bites the heads off pawns.

Maybe he is convinced they are prawns. That's a common mistake that people make. But Tue is an expert chess player. He should never confuse pieces for titbits. His teeth are worn down to stubs. But that doesn't hold his mouth back. His bite is worse than his bark.

Not that he actually barks very often. Only when he smells a wolf's scent. Sometimes his nostrils sniff furiously at Mun. But he hasn't barked at him yet. This suggests that Mun isn't a werewolf. Rumours get out of hand, however hairy. Best keep a tight grip on them!

Tue has been planning an elaborate trap. He has been moving his rooks cunningly. He prefers to move jackdaws and crows. But they fly away and never return. Rooks are content to remain as pieces. To slide smoothly along the chequered paths. Like abacus beads counting the enemy's losses.

He remembers a time quite long ago. He was a collector of rook feathers. Eventually he had enough for his purpose. He stitched them together into a cloak. It was softer than any other garment. It was warmer than his thickest coat. But he had to stop wearing it.

For some reason it affected his mind. He became overwhelmed with a strong desire. An urge to climb the tallest trees. To perch on the very highest branches. His parents probably would not have approved. Yet he remembered the advice they gave. Always be proud of your lofty ideals.

Yes, they had often told him that. But it is safer on the ground. Chess is much better for the bones. The view is arguably not as great. But fallen men have no working eyes. He abandoned his ideals and his cloak. Both gather dust in a secret cloakroom.

The third brooder is known as Wed. He is unmarried and has no plans. He only has eyes for chess pieces. He has superb knight vision, sure enough. He favours his knights over all others. He likes to jump pawns with them. He imagines the poor pawns' horrified faces.

And horse dung falling on their heads. Perhaps they will grow like garden plants. He has a large garden at home. But he has no interest in it. Chess is all he really cares about. If the pawns grew large, what then? They might become too heavy to lift.

Seven-sided chess is an unusual game. The board is totally chaotic with pieces. But the brothers only play this way. Seven brothers require a seven-sided board. The game is complex and sometimes unfair. Informal alliances can be made between players. The political aspects become even more important.

Always a loner, Wed never seeks allies. This might put him at a disadvantage. But his skill with knights is unparalleled. That is his not so secret strength. He moves them in totally unexpected patterns. They cause havoc among all his enemies. He draws considerable malignant attention to them.

But they evade danger like real horses. He stables them in a separate box. That's how much he loves those pieces. While he plays, his garden runs wild. There are tiny strawberries pecked by birds. If he ever did marry, what then? She would have to be very tolerant.

Don't underestimate the seriousness of this game. The winner will gain control of everything. His position will be elevated to emperor. He can even have another brother executed. But that is quite unlikely to happen. A six-sided board would be required. There is a new tournament every year.

It is simply an old family tradition. One game per year since time immemorial. Only one move a day, no more. Wed has made his move at last. He closes his eyes and waits patiently. He falls asleep and begins to dream. Horses crowd his mind, this time nightmares.

The fourth brooder is known as Thu. He is the joker of the brood. He's light hearted but still a brooder. How can such a thing be possible? With the darkest jokes, is the answer. Not dark as in cruel but melancholic. Thu's jokes will make one smile sadly.

A sad smile is a geometrical mystery. It has angles that can't be measured. It is too subtle and too unbearable. People smile sad smiles in strange seasons. Not in spring, summer, autumn or winter. Only in blabber, wail, sob and sniffle. Seasons parallel to the more familiar ones.

His favourite chess piece is the bishop. Perhaps because it's the one atheists hate. He has prepared special hats for them. Tiny items of headgear for his bishops. Not crash helmets or anything like that. Belled jester's caps with three diverging horns. Floppy and soft like his pendulous chin.

He is often asked about this chin. Why is it so pendulous on him? It helps his face to keep time. That's his answer and it's factually correct. The shadow of his nose keeps moving. This shadow is also a sly joker. It serves as a clock's hour hand.

Every twelve hours it points directly upwards. Jabs between his eyes like a finger. A smooth finger, flattened by a wheel. The wheel of a lorry carrying bishops. Thu imports his bishops from distant lands. He doesn't care for the native variety. He says they are stunted and greasy.

And that's true because of a misunderstanding. Chess players in this region are isolated. And ignorance sometimes holds hands with isolation. Amateurs will use cooks instead of rooks. Cooks that fry everything in olive oil. Even the pages of their recipe books. And they will dish up a bishop.

One of Thu's brothers is a cook. More about him in just a moment. The bishops go about their business diagonally. Just like jesters did in ancient courts. The nose shadow moves across his face. At last it jabs between his eyes. It is midnight and his ears chime.

The fifth brooder is known as Fri. He likes cooking his food in oil. Others say that is the crudest way. All the brothers are fat in truth. This fact must not be denied forever. Sitting motionless at a chessboard is unhealthy. Fri is the fattest of the brood.

He is sordid but not a rascal. His honest eyes blink like young grapes. Grapes that have been fried with garlic. He doesn't have a favourite chess piece. He is the only brother who doesn't. He treats them all equally, like olives. Or like grapes pretending to be olives.

This is a world of constant deception. Fri attempts to deceive all his opponents. Frequently he only manages to deceive himself. But seven-sided chess is an anomaly. A poor player can still be victor. There are so many opportunities for flukes. The board is too crowded and disordered.

Fog has been known to drift inside. It explores the hall with creamy tendrils. Cold and clammy, it drapes itself miserably. Like scarves chosen by a vindictive aunt. But Fri pretends it is cooking steam. He snorts as he watches it coil. Yes, constant deception is the only answer.

He shuts one eye to save it. Fog licks his other eyeball with languor. Green and scummy, it grapes itself morbidly. I mist you, the fog says lovingly. But this is only a literary device. Fog has tongues but can't speak words. Much less can it speak in tongues.

Who has ever really spoken in tongues? Why not speak in ears and cheeks? Speak in hands and listen in knees? A breeze enters to disperse the fog. Draughts are banned in the chess room! But this airy intrusion secretly pleases him. Now he can open his saved eye.

Save eyes long enough and interest accrues. Not just the interest of an ophthalmologist. That is how the banking system works. It is time for him to move. He castles his king and his rook. If the castle was a valid piece! Then that would be his favourite one.

The sixth brooder is known as Sat. He has never been known to stand. He travels everywhere in a special wheelchair. It's special because he made it himself. He constructed it from old kitchen utensils. Again the theme of cooking and food. But he is the least fat brother.

Clearly he must have a faster metabolism. Or maybe he burns calories another way. Through the furious motions of his eyebrows. Through the twitchings of his thin lips. Through the sneering of his wide nostrils. Sat is especially fond of his queen. He thinks of her as his wife.

Therefore he is very protective of her. He doesn't want to let her roam. But she is contemptuous of his concern. She is a strong and independent woman. She can bash bishops and annihilate knights. She can obliterate rooks and pulverise pawns. But enemy kings are her favourite prey.

One day she will turn on him. Sat knows this will be his tragedy. She will abruptly jump off the board. Land on his lap and attack him. His wheelchair is a steam-powered contraption. It contains the spirit of all kitchens. But he can't flee from his groin.

The vehicle will screech down the corridors. The other brothers will watch in amusement. But they will also feel some sympathy. They will gaze at their own queens. Their own groins will throb in rhythm. One day this will almost certainly happen. But let's remember the future isn't now.

We know that pawns can be promoted. Every single pawn is a potential queen. Therefore every pawn is a possible wife. But a queen isn't the only option. Pawns can be promoted to knights too. Also to rooks and bishops, both male. Sat is cautious about flirting with pawns.

At present his queen has wandered far. She hardly needs him to position her. She slides along under her own power. The truth is that she can't walk. She sits in her own miniature wheelchair. Sat constructed it from tiny kitchen utensils. And it is also powered by steam.

The seventh brooder is known as Sun. He has a bright and cheerful smile. He rarely tries to protect his king. He gives it a strong attacking role. This is an unusual method in chess. The result is that he usually loses. Yet nothing will wipe away his grin.

But one year he was the winner. Chess analysts still study that curious game. His king rampaged through the massed ranks. His opponents got in each other's way. Possibly they were blinded by his smile. He cleans his teeth every three hours. He checks Thu's face for the time.

Sun is slightly bored by the game. This is his deepest and darkest secret. The secret's darkness doesn't affect his smile. He wants to resign and go home. But it is too early for that. People would gossip and say unpleasant things. Yes, there's an audience in the hall.

They already think Mon is a werewolf. They already think Tue bites pawn heads. They already think Wed is a solipsist. They already think Thu is a clock. They already think Fri is a globule. They already think Sat is a cuckold. Sun alone can save the family reputation.

They merely say he is a grinner. The reputation rests entirely on his shoulders. But he yearns to shrug it off. Surely there must be another escape route? What if he managed to fall ill? But the rate of play is slow. One move per day is the rule.

He would get better before his turn. No one would have noticed his sickness. That method simply won't work at all. He hopes that inspiration will strike soon. Gazes around the board at his brothers. Then he realises they are equally bored. And now it is his move again.

Sometimes we push ourselves beyond our limits. Sun's king has reached the furthest square. And Sun is absolutely ready to finish. He moves his king off the board. It takes one of the Doric columns. The column topples over as it surrenders. The roof comes down, the curtain too.

$$\geq 2n+1$$

Author's Note

I have mentioned the OuLiPo grouping of experimental fiction writers. OuLiPo can be rendered in English as 'Workshop of Potential Literatures' and is less a school than a series of methods for writing original and unusual fiction. These methods are usually based on mathematical constraints. Often such constraints are not dissimilar from those that poets have been imposing on themselves for centuries, but they can be considerably more complex too, and are applied both to poetry and prose. The most famous OuLiPo constraint is the lipogram, which requires a writer to create a text devoid of a specific letter, the most challenging omission being a vowel, especially 'e'. The remarkable polymath Georges Perec wrote an entire novel without this vowel.

Although at first it may seem pointless to attempt and realise such a schema, in fact there are good reasons behind the need to push the limits of form in this manner. Real life is also a lipogram of sorts, in which the absent element might be an aspect, possession or experience rather than a letter. A tale written without using a chosen vowel is possibly a close analogue to such a real world situation as a life lived without love or money or influence. This is why I insist that there is more to OuLiPo than mere indulgence and contrivance. A constrained literary reality has the potential to mirror our own reality more exactly, even poignantly, than an entirely free fictional portrait can. We are bound by the framing rules of the cosmos, just the same as OuLiPo prose.

There are many other OuLiPo constraints. N+7 is a particularly entertaining one, in which all the nouns of an existing text are shifted forwards or backwards by seven places in any dictionary that might be at hand. 'There is no jam in the pot' may become 'There is no Japanese in the potato' or 'There is no joke in the precedent' or a variety of other startling statements depending on the dictionary. One is encouraged to invent new constraints too, and in the text that follows this is what I have done. I call my constraint ≥2n+1 (greater or equal to 2n plus one) and it creates story grids that can be read coherently across every row and down every column and along the main diagonals.

Those are the deliberate tales in the grids but unintentional ones might exist on other diagonals, in reverse directions on columns and rows, and in non-linear meanderings throughout the grids. The 8x8 grid called 'I Entered the Forest at Midnight' was the first to be written and was translated into Greek a few years ago and published in an OuLiPo anthology, but it has never appeared in English until now. The text that accompanies it serves the same function as this author's note but attempts to be explanatory in a more poetic manner. A poetic manner for explanations is now deemed irregular.

The 2x2 to 7x7 grids that together form one quasi-story called 'Boiling the Kettle' proved trickier to construct but taught me much about how careful one must be with tenses and plurals and homonyms in order to get the intersections right. The several irregular grids of 'The Careful Plottings of my Enamoured Heart' are an attempt to break free from the chessboard restriction, play with asymmetry, and make more use of the potential of the diagonals. I perceive a Japanese flavour to some of the results, although Bashō and the other classical haiku poets might disagree if they were alive to see them. We often believe we are being Japanese when in fact we are merely being bumblebees, ill-at-ease or cottage cheese. This is an absurd but lyrical truth.

And one of the many hazards of the experimental author's life.

I Entered the Forest at Midnight

I entered the forest at midnight	after winding my hallway clock	so it wouldn't run down in my absence	like a slave worked too hard	while I went to investigate the scream	I had heard from my open window	as my wife waited patiently for me	in the alcove in the hallway
feeling braver than usual	when the moon had just risen	I tied up the untamed dragon	with a frayed rope and vital help	of a rampant genie	the sound of a distant golden lute	offering liquid beauty to	an old woman sat drinking
with a spring in my step	I decided to practice jumping	over the hill behind my house	I dropped into a marsh	on top of a will o' the wisp	and it filled me with a desire to	take it home and keep it in	a bottle half full of brandy
as tightly coiled as my pocket galaxy I ran	for joy in the style of a child but	hung it from a hook-shaped cloud	but I couldn't see where I walked	I had only pure sound to help me	learn the identity of the player	the drum that troubled the night	as the galaxy cooled in the sky
feeling youthful as I dodged the tree trunks	I forgot I am too old now and	like the pendulum of a gigantic clock	a large branch swung itself at my head	and I groped my way like a blind man	so I strained my eyes as hard as I could	while the stars whirled around my eyes	and the planets danced their ellipses
dressed in the wrong clothes	twisting my ankles and bruising my knees	when there was no time left to tell	and I wandered off the path	through mud as thick as treacle	until the dull glow appeared ahead	as cool as two glow-worms	like lovers who are also spies
with boots that were too tight	I had to hobble instead of walk	and the world seemed a safer place	because I could not hurry into danger	but I was chasing an enigma of sighs	and I saw the musical vibration	the flame I was seeking	around the sentimental object that was the sun
but happier than I had been for ages	for the remainder of the long hours	now the scaly monster was no longer free	I decided to forget my duties and chores	and hoping to catch the dream	in fact a sunbeam caught in a spider web	I cupped instead in my eager fingers	the burning heart of the woman I loved

The chessboard is a landscape for games, problems, dreams. Sixty-four squares on which kings and queens, nobles and commoners can mate and slay, and die in their turn. It is the perfect battlefield or theatre for other kinds of adventures too: the strange journey, the supernatural romance, the monstrous encounter. In this sublime grid, whole libraries of novels might be condensed, lengthy stories powdered like spices and sample grains positioned next to each other to give an enticing flavour of the fantasy worlds they represent.

These are potential novels rather than actual. They probably will never be written in full. More important is the way they interact with all the other stories and possibilities. In fact, the fulcrum points, the junctions, between the tales *are* the tales; they comprise the totality of the grid. There is no sample, no extract or description that belongs to just one story. Every snippet of text contributes to at least two tales; and a few belong coherently to three. The incidents of our lives are surely like this in the real world, never isolated.

The tales are read from left to right, and also from up to down. Thus there are eight rows and eight columns of separate stories. There is also a tale running along the main diagonal from top left to bottom right, and this was the first to be written, the foundation for all the others. This makes a total of seventeen stories. Additionally there are perhaps half a dozen accidental tales on some of the other diagonals, smaller adventures that make enough sense but not through intention. They designed or evolved themselves on their own.

An ideal story grid of this kind would be arranged in such a way that tales could be read in *all* directions and *every* tale would be beautiful and true. I feel immense relief that I shall not be the one to attempt this task. A computer might be better suited for the vast effort. But why stop with a chessboard in only two dimensions? The interconnected tales could take place on cubes and polyhedra, and even tesseracts and other forms that belong to higher geometries. Journeys, love and monsters will surely still be valid themes.

Boiling the Kettle

Boiling the kettle	the steam billowed
I arranged the cups	on my fevered brow

I drank the hot tea	while reading the newspaper	from beginning to end
after I ate the biscuit	in three large gulps	the volcano erupted
covered with chillies	I digested the bad news	and burned my tongue

This isolated castle	near the mountain of flame	raised by my great grandfather and	looming over the glassy plain
a maze in all but name	that has been my home	nurtured on a supernatural diet	of smoothly fused green rock
only with her and her burning eyes	I play chess in the flickering glare	since I was a child	the red haired woman
I found the way	of forest fires	a valuable lesson	I wish never to forget

Setting sail	in the morning	when all are asleep	I leave my life behind	seeking another
with unseemly haste	from the shore	the moonlight fades	like the smile of the only	woman that I can adore
I catch the wind	with a net on a pole	I am uncertain about	lips that sigh and devour	like a caged beast
blowing from the north	the stranger greets me	the dryness of wit and	my final destination	heavy on my mind
colder than a hateful eye	with a menacing wave	the sea breaks over me	and a mermaid kisses me	but it is not you

A late arrival	at the station	I am stranded	in a high city	alone and thinking	how nice a coffee would be
tomorrow night	is better than	next week	for the climbing	of the old peach tree	in bird streaked moonlight
far distant	in the cafe	an early start	plants a new hope	every memory that	warms a night more
people gathering	to wait for a bus	the only escape	if the destination	turns out to be better	than our current plight
in a hope of greeting me	that will never come	for the stranger who is	beyond the mountain	is a wrong one	that only seems to be right
with offers of food	when I am most thirsty	the person who feeds me	is kind but unhelpful	and I am saddened	said the migrating bird

Better not to know	who is calling	on the telephone	in the morning	after a night of	too many tales	in case it is bad news
how many times when	the secrets of	a whisper about	the girl devoted to	passion and excess	turn out to be lies	on the radio
hurrying to his true	love across town	your best friend	quiet hails a taxi but	the wise man will	drive without music or	turn it off
calling out of respect	this bright morning	his wife asks what	if you prefer to	cool his feet and	dip them in hot sauce	before eating
for his old faith	if it is not a young	wine he will	open the bottle and	resist the insight that	it will fail to soften	the hard dry rice
the monk is a drunk	man with more zest	forget to offer	drink it all down	pedalling to generate	life is always an	unwise decision
more or less	than discretion	to the hostess	please don't wait for her	current is a weird vice	essential to power	unboiled kettle.

The Careful Plottings of My Enamoured Heart

In the forest	am I a phoenix	scorched with lust
there is a blue bear	sitting in a pear tree	too hairy to win
let us be friends	said the bird that burned	a trio of girls

like mutant fruits	for supper today	the peculiar chef asked
the beating hearts were	ready to drop on	the heads that rule
in their squat jars	luxurious laps and	unsuspecting men

my cape is brand new	I found it yesterday	among the body parts	down the lift shaft
like a glass of juice	made from moonlight	in the laboratory	a hand of odd fingers
it spills around me	the babbling brook that	I reach within	to pluck out a fish
a friendly large wave	said hello to the cats	I stroke them gently	and tickle myself pink

plots thicken	as hair thins out	on devious heads			
mud pools tremble	and so do soups	the tusks glisten	the restless hands	determined girls	during the invasion
when elephants appear	we whisper more gently	and the trunks	reach for branches	squeeze the ripe fruit	of stranded parachutists
			of growing trees	my dear friend said	cut down none at all

		the	moon			
	catch	endless	beams	tonight			
when	reflections	of	surf	gleam	are	not	enough
	are	fish			smiles	rotting	
	never	known			always	broken	
the	careful	plottings	of	my	enamoured	heart	collapse
		within	tigers	course	softly		
			beware	changes			

	plays tunes	with spoons	long after		
	quick now	dig out	the bowl		
the dog	barks soft	the cave	is full	of his	sad echoes
is back			slowly sinks	dead hands	gently stir
and my		sending her	the letter	written on	blue paper
pond is		far away	deep down		
lapped by	salty sea	sweet ships			
his tongue	drools over	the girl			

			the big	climax to	all scenes			
			final birth	days are	terribly dramatic			
			where are	long nights	here at			
my heart	beats faster	after visiting	the doctors		the theatres	last and	best show	has begun
and mind	the gap	when alighting				first men	I am	to be
are absent	friends still	before arrival	fondly re-membered		quite alone	in London	rather serious	too excited
			easily forgot	eyes shut	at last			
			come and	see how	I sigh			
			go together	I fall	very deeply			

	juggle	tasks		kiss	only	
keep	your	promise		or	leave	me
bouncing	balls	busy		love	the	fly
higher	in	days	to	make	room	above
	the				when	
	great				it's	
	halls				not	
	of				too	
than	the	cities	will	expand	soon	endless
the	castle	crumbles		changes	to	green
fence	of	truth		angels	offend	oceans
	mirth	persists		bless	us	

do you relish	buying an ape	from a market			opened my mind	raided a gherkin jar	I really would
an unbearable urge	to eat papaya	I escaped with	two other prisoners	into the jungle	picked the fruit	and stuffed myself	like a sofa
for a purge	chopped very finely	salad at night			picked the nose	I like long ones	I'll buy it

the warmth	more in the mind	than on the skin
and the horns	of the crescent moon	hooking the night
of the holy cow	singing of songs	is not enough

to dry her tears	I fan her face	with an old tapestry
I peg her	on my shoulder	a stuffed parrot
on a washing line	there are cobwebs	that sparkle

like dew or	men who claim to	vanish with the dawn
drops of sweat	like pearls	sold in the market
on a god's brow	fruits they are	of unripe wisdom

I walked	down the	hill slopes
just where	long paths	are steep
it is good	for you	to be near

never stop	singing to	the moon
uncle said	your aunt	is mad
and thus	she eats	bananas

the sky	you and	even I
because	we shall	walk still
they are	friends be	what may

two hearts	are not	in love
on two	clear days	despite all
sleeves	can be	problems

we say	hello to	ghosts
about that	snow	drift
today	smile	aimlessly

Vestigial Appendix

For lazy readers, here are the microfictions set out in a more conventional format. This also enables me to add punctuation where necessary to make each single line story easier to read.

I Entered the Forest at Midnight

<u>Main Diagonal</u>

- I entered the forest at midnight when the moon had just risen over the hill behind my house, but I couldn't see where I walked and I groped my way like a blind man until the dull glow appeared ahead, the flame I was seeking, the burning heart of the woman I loved.

<u>Columns</u>

- I entered the forest at midnight feeling braver than usual; with a spring in my step as tightly coiled as my pocket galaxy I ran feeling youthful as I dodged the tree trunks, dressed in the wrong clothes with boots that were too tight but happier than I had been for ages.

- After winding my hallway clock when the moon had just risen, I decided to practice jumping for joy in the style of a child, but I forgot I am now too old and twisting my ankles and bruising my knees I had to hobble instead of walk for the remainder of the long hours.

- So it wouldn't run down in my absence, I tied up the untamed dragon over the hill behind my house, hung it from a hook-shaped cloud like the pendulum of a gigantic clock when there was no time left to tell and the world seemed a safer place now the scaly monster was no longer free.

- Like a slave worked too hard, with a frayed rope and vital help, I dropped into a marsh but I couldn't see where I walked; a large branch swung itself at my head and I wandered off the path; because I could not hurry into danger I decided to forget my duties and chores.

- While I went to investigate the scream of a rampant genie on top of a will o' the wisp, I had only pure sound to help me and I groped my way like a blind man through mud as thick as treacle, but I was chasing an enigma of sighs and hoping to catch the dream.

- I had heard from my open window the sound of a distant golden lute and it filled me with a desire to learn the identity of the player, so I strained my eyes as hard as I could until the dull glow appeared ahead and I saw the musical vibration; in fact a sunbeam caught in a spider web.

- As my wife waited patiently for me, offering liquid beauty to take it home and keep it in the drum that troubled the night while the stars whirled around, my eyes as cool as two glow worms; the flame I was seeking I cupped instead in my eager fingers.

- In the alcove in the hallway an old woman sat drinking a bottle half full of brandy as the galaxy cooled in the sky and the planets danced their ellipses like lovers who are also spies around the sentimental object that was the sun, the burning heart of the woman I loved.

Rows

- I entered the forest at midnight after winding my hallway clock so it wouldn't run down in my absence like a slave worked too hard while I went to investigate the scream I had heard from my open window as my wife waited patiently for me in the alcove in the hallway.

- Feeling braver than usual when the moon had just risen, I tied up the untamed dragon with a frayed rope and vital help of a rampant genie; the sound of a distant golden lute offering liquid beauty to an old woman sat drinking.

- With a spring in my step I decided to practice jumping over the hill behind my house; I dropped into a marsh on top of a will o' the wisp and it filled me with a desire to take it home and keep it in a bottle half full of brandy.

- As tightly coiled as my pocket galaxy I ran for joy in the style of a child but hung it from a hook-shaped cloud, but I couldn't see where I walked, I had only pure sound to help me learn the identity of the player, the drum that troubled the night as the galaxy cooled in the sky.

- Feeling youthful as I dodged the tree trunks I forgot I am too old now, and like the pendulum of a gigantic clock a large branch swung itself at my head and I groped my way like a blind man, so I strained my eyes as hard as I could while the stars whirled around my eyes and the planets danced their ellipses.

- Dressed in the wrong clothes, twisting my ankles and bruising my knees, when there was no time left to tell and I wandered off the path through mud as thick as treacle until the dull glow appeared ahead as cool as two glow worms like lovers who are also spies.

- With boots that were too tight I had to hobble instead of walk and the world seemed a safer place because I could not hurry into danger, but I was chasing an enigma of sighs and I saw the musical vibration, the flame I was seeking, around the sentimental object that was the sun.

- But happier than I had been for ages, for the remainder of the long hours, now the scaly monster was no longer free, I decided to forget my duties and chores and hoping to catch the dream, in fact a sunbeam caught in a spider web, I cupped instead in my eager fingers the burning heart of the woman I loved.

Boiling the Kettle

2x2

Main Diagonal

- Boiling the kettle on my fevered brow.

Columns

- Boiling the kettle I arranged the cups.
- The steam billowed on my fevered brow.

Rows

- Boiling the kettle, the steam billowed.
- I arranged the cups on my fevered brow.

3x3

Main Diagonal

- I drank the hot tea in three large gulps and burned my tongue.

Columns

- I drank the hot tea after I ate the biscuit covered with chillies.
- While reading the newspaper, in three large gulps I digested the bad news.
- From beginning to end, the volcano erupted and burned my tongue.

<u>Rows</u>

- I drank the hot tea while reading the newspaper from beginning to end.

- After I ate the biscuit in three large gulps the volcano erupted.

- Covered with chillies, I digested the bad news and burned my tongue.

4x4

<u>Main Diagonal</u>

- This isolated castle that has been my home since I was a child I wish never to forget.

<u>Columns</u>

- This isolated castle, a maze in all but name; only with her and her burning eye I found the way.

- Near the mountain of flame that has been my home, I play chess in the flickering glare of forest fires.

- Raised by my great-grandfather, nurtured on a supernatural diet since I was a child, a valuable lesson.

- Looming over the glassy plain of smoothly fused green rock, the red haired woman I wish never to forget.

<u>Rows</u>

- This isolated castle near the mountain of flame, raised by my great-grandfather and looming over the glassy plain.

- A maze in all but name that has been my home, nurtured on a supernatural diet of smoothly fused green rock.

- Only with her and her burning eyes, I play chess in the flickering glare since I was a child, the red haired woman.

- I found the way of forest fires a valuable lesson I wish never to forget.

5x5

<u>Main Diagonal</u>

- Setting sail from the shore I am uncertain about my final destination but it is not you.

Columns

- Setting sail with unseemly haste, I catch the wind blowing from the north, colder than a hateful eye.

- In the morning from the shore with a net on a pole the stranger greets me with a menacing wave.

- When all are asleep, the moonlight fades, I am uncertain about the dryness of wit and the sea breaks over me.

- I leave my life behind like the smile of the only lips that sigh and devour my final destination and a mermaid kisses me.

- Seeking another woman that I can adore like a caged beast heavy on my mind, but it is not you.

Rows

- Setting sail in the morning when all are asleep, I leave my life behind, seeking another.

- With unseemly haste, from the shore the moonlight fades, like the smile of the only woman that I can adore.

- I catch the wind with a net on a pole, I am uncertain about lips that sigh and devour like a caged beast.

- Blowing from the north, the stranger greets me, the dryness of wit and my final destination heavy on my mind.

- Colder than a hateful eye, with a menacing wave the sea breaks over me and a mermaid kisses me, but it is not you.

6x6

Main Diagonal

- A late arrival is better than an early start if the destination is a wrong one, said the migrating bird.

Columns

- A late arrival tomorrow night, far distant people gathering in a hope of greeting me with offers of food.

- At the station is better than in the café to wait for a bus that will never come when I am most thirsty.

- I am stranded, next week an early start, the only escape for the stranger who is the person who feeds me.

- In a high city, for the climbing plants a new hope, if the destination beyond the mountain is kind but unhelpful.

- Alone and thinking of the old peach tree, every memory that turns out to be better is a wrong one and I am saddened.

- How nice a coffee would be in bird streaked moonlight, warms a night more than our current plight that only seems to be right, said the migrating bird.

Rows

- A late arrival at the station, I am stranded in a high city, alone and thinking how nice a coffee would be.

- Tomorrow night is better than next week for the climbing of the old peach tree in bird streaked moonlight.

- Far distant, in the café an early start plants a new hope, every memory that warms a night more.

- People gathering to wait for a bus, the only escape if the destination turns out to be better than our current plight.

- In a hope of greeting me that will never come, for the stranger who is beyond the mountain is a wrong one that only seems to be right.

- With offers of food when I am most thirsty, the person who feeds me is kind but unhelpful, and I am saddened, said the migrating bird.

7x7

Main Diagonal

- Better not to know the secrets of your best friend if you prefer to resist the insight that life is always an unboiled kettle.

Columns

- Better not to know how many times, when hurrying to his true calling out of respect for his old faith, the monk is drunk, more or less.

- Who is calling the secrets of love across town this bright morning, if it is not a young man with more zest than discretion?

- On the telephone, a whisper about your best friend, his wife asks what wine he will forget to offer to the hostess.

- In the morning, the girl devoted to quiet hails a taxi, but if you prefer to open the bottle and drink it all down please don't wait for her.

- After a night of passion and excess, the wise man will cool his feet and resist the insight that pedalling to generate current is a weird vice.

- Too many tales turn out to be lies, drive without music or dip them in hot sauce, it will fail to soften, life is always an essential to power.

- In case it is bad news on the radio, turn it off before eating the hard dry rice, unwise decision, unboiled kettle.

<u>Rows</u>

- Better not to know who is calling on the telephone in the morning after a night of too many tales in case it is bad news.

- How many times when the secrets of a whisper about the girl devoted to passion and excess turn out to be lies on the radio?

- Hurrying to his true love across town, your best friend, quiet, hails a taxi but the wise man will drive without music or turn it off.

- Calling out of respect this bright morning, his wife asks what if you prefer to cool his feet and dip them in hot sauce before eating.

- For his odd faith, if it is not a young wine, he will open the bottle and resist the insight that it will fail to soften the hard dry rice.

- The monk is a drunk man with more zest, forget to offer, drink it all down, pedalling to generate life is always an unwise decision.

- More or less than discretion to the hostess, please don't wait for her, current is a weird vice essential to power unboiled kettle.

The Careful Plottings of My Enamoured Heart

There are too many microfictions in too many different directions on these grids to make it worthwhile listing them here in a systematic fashion. In this story there is more scope for the creation of accidental tales, of which many make sense, many don't, and some make a sort of semi-sense and thus are the most intriguing of all. There are also greater opportunities for stories to be read in a meandering fashion across the grids. For the sake of providing a sample, four random microfictions taken from the nine grids are as follows:

- In the forest, sitting in a pear tree, a trio of girls like mutant fruits, ready to drop on unsuspecting men.

- Plots thicken and so do soups and the trunks of growing trees.

- The warmth of the crescent moon is not enough to dry her tears on my shoulder that sparkle like dew or like pearls of unripe wisdom.

- I walked down the hill slopes just where paths are steep, it is good for you to be near the sky, you and even I, because we shall walk still, they are friends, be what may.

I hope that these story grids will catch on and that $\geq 2n+1$ will become an official constraint in the OuLiPo battery of techniques. Experimentation with form is less popular than it once was, as I have already said, but it is still fun, and invigorating, to me certainly, and surely to others too.

Logical Love

Author's Note

The following story is a logico-erotic tale in which the permutations of the sexual acts are based on the workings of logic gates. It was originally written for the OuLiPo anthology in Greek that I have already mentioned, but the editor preferred 'I Entered the Forest at Midnight' because he had no familiarity with Boolean Algebra. It might appear at first glance that logic and eroticism have nothing in common, and this perception might be completely true. All the more reason to attempt to combine them in an experimental fiction!

The art of the erotic story is a highly developed one and it is not a fictional form that particularly suits my abilities. Indeed, when I consider my body of work, it is the erotic pieces that I often most regret writing. Or rather I seem to be incapable of creating erotic situations in fiction that are genuinely arousing. They tend to the absurd and whimsical instead. However, with this story, I am on safer ground. The precise workings of the logic gates determine what occurs and there can be no deviation from the required combinations that create each particular sexual input and orgasmic output.

Boolean Amours

AND

The bed is cool and long in the shadows. If neither Anna nor Bernal achieve satisfaction, the act of love is a failure. It is also a failure if Anna or Bernal achieve satisfaction without the other doing so. Only if they both achieve satisfaction at the same time, or within a very short time of each other, will the coupling be said to have had a positive outcome.

OR

In a small red boat on a wide but shallow green lake. It is only necessary for one of the partners, Alice or Boris, to reach orgasm for the encounter to be deemed worthwhile and beautiful. If they both manage to do so, that is fine too, it is excellent in fact, but nothing depends on this single eventuality. The ecstasy of one is certainly enough.

NOT

The monastery cell is cold to the eye but not to the touch, for the stones have kept the heat of the slanting afternoon sun that sliced its beams on the iron bars of the narrow window. If Benedict has an orgasm as a result of his fumblings, then he has failed. His mind and soul are not strong enough to master the flesh. If there is no orgasm, then he is a success.

NAND

Amber and Bryan are nearing the end of their relationship. Only this could explain the situation they find themselves in. If neither of them achieves satisfaction, the act of love is a success. It is also a success if either achieves it without the other. But if both achieve it, the act has failed. They turn from each other and scowl, back to damp back, on a sagging mattress.

NOR

At an even later stage of disaffection, Amanda and Bron live apart. But occasionally they visit each other in order to claim a previously communal possession that is shared no longer, perhaps a shirt or kitchen utensil. Inspired by revenge they will fuck on the sofa. Only if neither achieves orgasm are they satisfied with the experience, this validation of bitterness.

XOR

The red boat might be far out on the green lake, but on the sandy shore a couple are swimming in each other. Abigail is the sister of Alice, Brand is the brother of Boris. They have been left behind here and have taken advantage of the privacy to undress and explore each other with passion. But unfamiliarity is disruptive. Only if one of them reaches orgasm do they feel capable of breaking apart with smiles of contentment.

XNOR

It is all or nothing for Anastasia and Bleys. They met in a crowded market one day, eyes touching across the hills of fruit and electrical plugs. They are equals in everything, a nation of two in a world of tangled fates. Lovemaking for them is as democratic a process as any other. If neither reaches orgasm or if both do, there is triumph, a beautiful symmetry. If only one does, there is defeat, a fatal distortion of togetherness.

Benedict, when the nights grow longer in winter, is able to speculate on matters far beyond the nourishment of his faith. Or perhaps not, for logic is a subject he must study in the daytime. It occurs to him, on an abstract level alone, for the mental images produced do not excite him now, that any of the above sexual situations can be represented by a combination of couples exactly like Amanda and Bron.

NOT (NOR)

If Amanda decides unilaterally to pleasure herself and Bron at the same time with her hands, adjusting speed, rhythm and pressure to ensure total parity, the resulting double orgasm will be rated as one failure. Conversely a double failure to orgasm will be rated as one success. This is how that couple replicate the situation Benedict experienced earlier in his cell.

OR (NOR)

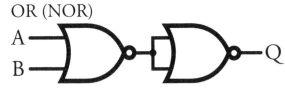

If Andrea and Ben, a couple exactly like Amanda and Bron, engage in intercourse they will do so in the hope that neither of them achieves satisfaction. Once they have finished with penetration, Andrea can attempt to pleasure herself and Ben in the same way that Amanda did with Bron, using her hands, and the end result will be the same as with Alice and Boris. If Andrea or Ben orgasm with or without the other, the outcome is a positive experience, and the encounter is only a failure if neither does so.

AND (NOR)

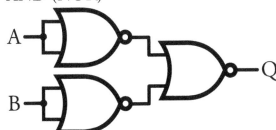

Annabel and Bertolt sit on chairs facing each other. They are trying to pleasure themselves and each other at the same time. This takes a remarkable level of coordination, for there are always two hands on each sexual organ. When they have finished, with varied results, for perhaps one achieved orgasm without the other, or both did, or neither, they fall on each other and fuck without love. They are a couple exactly like Amanda and Bron or Andrea and Ben. But the fucking produces results identical to those of Anna and Bernal on their cool bed in a room above a cobbled street. Only if they orgasm together will they be content.

NAND (NOR)

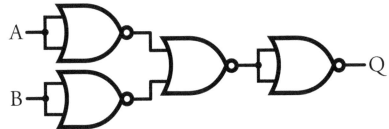

Alexia and Bertrand do the same thing that Annabel and Bertolt did, but seated on beanbags rather than chairs.

They like to be comfortable and when they have finished using their hands on each other, they fall upon each other and he penetrates her, and when that is also finished, they resume pleasuring with hands alone, or rather she takes over this duty. The consequences are the same as those of Amber and Bryan, ultimately selfish and defensive. One beanbag splits open and disgorges its beans like fossil tears.

XOR (NOR)

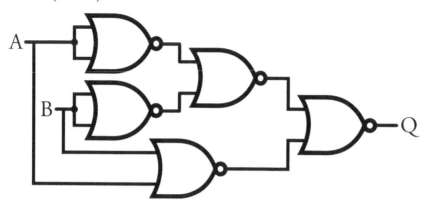

The ingenuity of perversity never fails to astonish the innocent eye and the effort involved seems to be greater than any possible reward. The contortions that Amelia and Bob are now attempting necessitate an exactitude of positioning and timing that would do credit to the most seasoned circus performers. Both partners are pleasuring themselves and each other at the same time with their hands, but they are also actively engaged in giving carnal satisfaction to another couple entwined with them. This extraneous couple appears to be Amanda and Bron but it is difficult to be certain in the dim lighting of the deserted hotel lobby. When Amelia and Bob finish with each other, they fuck. The other couple, briefly abandoned, wait for the conjoining to be completed and when they are ready again the quartet proceed to pleasure another couple, who might be Andrea and Ben. This double threesome finally results in an outcome. It is a complex sequence prone to propagation delays and yet the output is only the same as that of Abigail and Brand on their simple sandy shore.

XNOR (NOR)

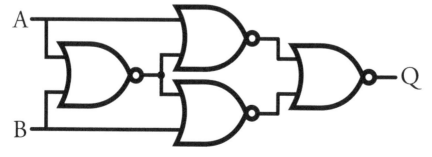

Ada is enjoying two men at the same time and one of them is her regular partner, Bill, who is enjoying two women at once, one of them being Ada and the other Adriana. The extra man enjoyed by Ada is Brutus. When Ada and Bill finish with each other, they help to pleasure Adriana and Brutus, who physically do not touch. When they have finished doing this, Ada and Bill fall back languidly and allow Adriana and Brutus finally to join together. Oddly enough this brand new couple create a fierce loyalty as they fuck, a solidarity of bliss the same as that of Anastasia and Bleys, who first met in the market of this very city, where the public clocks now strike midnight.

Benedict accepts that messy relationships and complicated geometries of lust can precisely replicate the effects of pure and simple love. There is a small time delay as the multiple orgasms, or multiple lack of orgasms, in the complex couplings modify each other, cancel themselves out, amplify or reverse the sensations. He sits in the cloister gardens and the pilgrims are gathered around him in a wise semicircle.

He tells them that the original seven situations can be represented not only by combinations of couples like Amanda and Bron, but also by couples like Amber and Bryan. He has worked out the logic of this too. A stick is in his hand and he draws patterns in the dust. But these pilgrims are not expected to demonstrate the orgasmic sequences now. It is getting late. They will pray instead for peace of mind.

Prayers follow no logic and the outputs can never be deduced from the inputs. But peace of mind does come. Anna, Alice, Amber, Amanda, Abigail, Anastasia, Andrea, Annabel, Alexia, Amelia, Ada and Adriana form one half of the twilight semicircle, while Bernal, Boris, Bryan, Bron, Brand, Bleys, Ben, Bertolt, Bertrand, Bob, Bill and Brutus form the other half, and Benedict is the unfucked focal point.

Night falls over the Boolean monastery.
And lovers elsewhere activate the gates of paradise.

Lightning Source UK Ltd.
Milton Keynes UK
UKHW05f1109080518
322264UK00007B/35/P